POOKA

Alison Murray

ORCHARD

Nina lived
on the ninth
floor of a tall
building
in a
**BIG,
LOUD**
city.

Nina loved her home,
but deep inside she
had a secret wish.

It started as a niggle
in her tummy,

then it grew to an ache in her heart.

Before she knew it, Nina's wish had grown too big to keep inside.

"I wish this place could be different," she shouted.

But her small voice was lost in the big roar of the city.

Feeling defeated, Nina sat on her favourite bench in the tiny city park. "What can I do?" she wondered. "I am small, and small things don't count."

"Oh, small things count alright," said a voice. "EVERYTHING starts with something small."

Nina looked around. There was no one there!

Then out from under a leaf stepped
the strangest little creature Nina had
ever seen. He had big, bright eyes
and Nina could see right through
his body, like he was nothing
more than mist.

"Are you a ghost?" whispered Nina.

"I am a Pooka,"
said the creature.

"What's a Pooka?" asked Nina.

"AH HA!" he cried.
"I will show you."

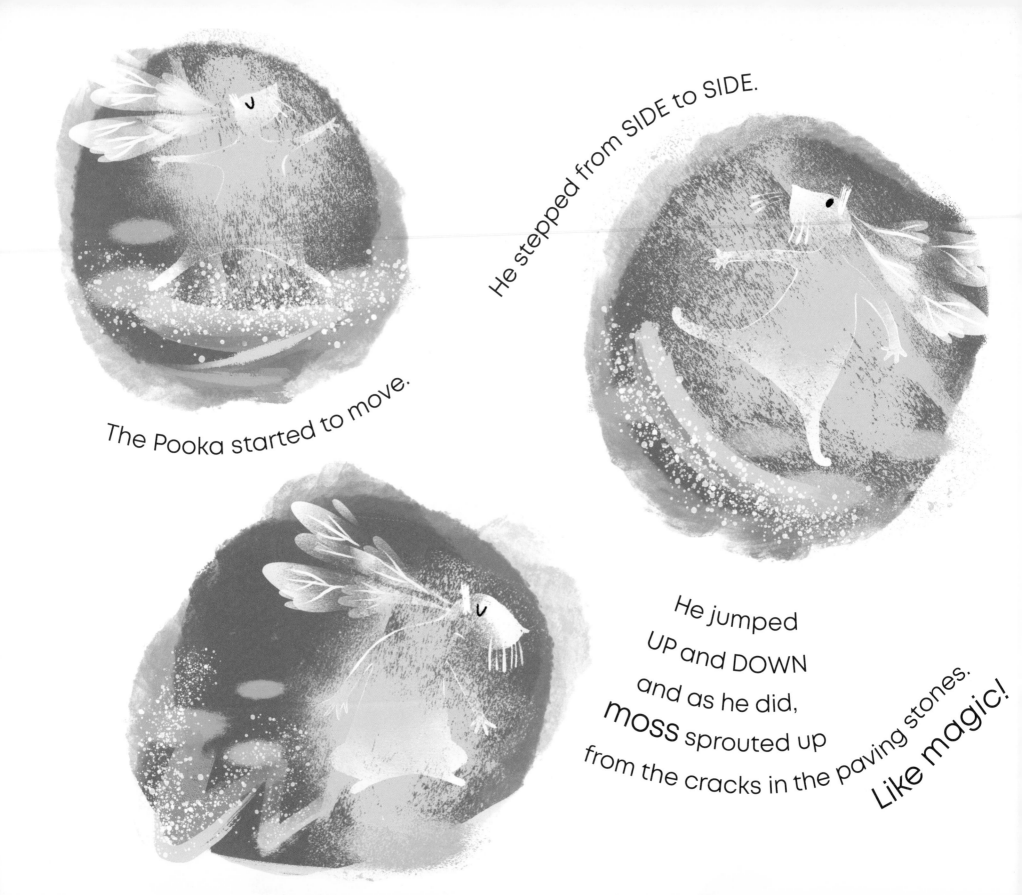

The Pooka started to move.

He stepped from SIDE to SIDE.

He jumped
UP and DOWN
and as he did,
moss sprouted up
from the cracks in the paving stones.
Like magic!

"Pookas can
dance the
Foozy dance,"
he explained.

"And when we do…"

". . . nature dances with us."

Nina saw that the Pooka had grown bigger.
He seemed a little less see-through too.

He placed a tiny acorn in Nina's hand.
"Now it's your turn," he said.

Nina knelt down and pressed it into the earth
between the paving stones and . . .

WHOOSH!

Up, up,
up grew
a mighty
oak tree.

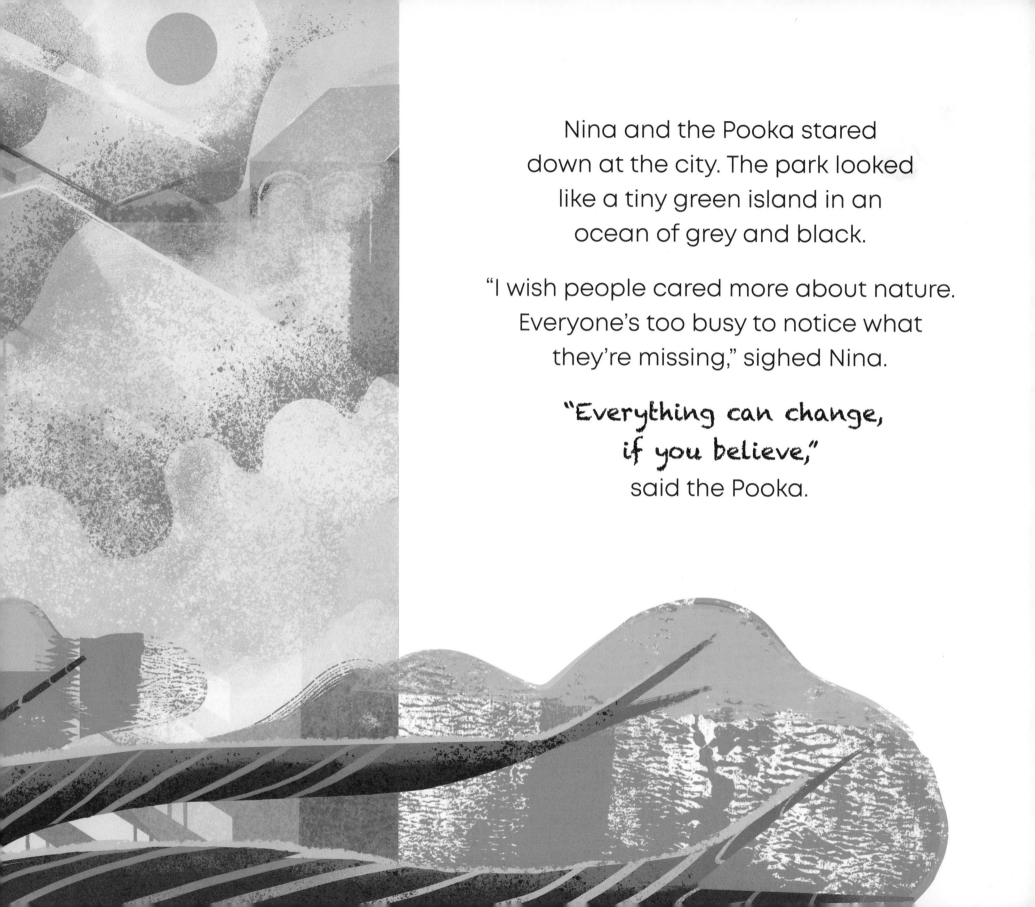

Nina and the Pooka stared
down at the city. The park looked
like a tiny green island in an
ocean of grey and black.

"I wish people cared more about nature.
Everyone's too busy to notice what
they're missing," sighed Nina.

**"Everything can change,
if you believe,"**
said the Pooka.

"I believe!" said Nina, taking the Pooka's soft paw.

"Remember,
everything starts small,"
said the Pooka, giving Nina
a handful of seeds.

Then they started
to dance.

They danced throughout the city,
and around the supermarket
an orchard grew.

They danced over bridges,
and bright trailing blossoms
spilled over the walls.

They danced under
a bright yellow moon.

Long grasses and wildflowers
grew in alleyways. Life
sprang from everywhere
and joined the
magical dance.

As the sun began to rise, they sat on a grassy rooftop, looking out over the transformed city.

"It's beautiful," Nina whispered.

The Pooka was big now – big and warm and cuddly. Nina felt her eyelids growing heavy.

As she drifted off to sleep, she heard the Pooka say,

"Even the tiniest seed can make a difference. If you believe."

When she woke, Nina was back in her own bed. "I must have imagined it all," she thought.

Then a blast of clean, fresh air billowed through the curtain and she heard *quiet*. Just the buzz of a bee and the song of a bird . . .

. . . and she ran to the window.

For Gracie Martha, Roslyn
and all the lockdown babies the world over.
A. M.

ORCHARD BOOKS
First published in Great Britain in 2022 by The Watts Publishing Group

10 8 6 4 2 1 3 5 7 9

Text and illustrations © Alison Murray 2022
The moral rights of the author have been asserted.
All rights reserved.
A CIP catalogue record for this book is available from the British Library.
ISBNs: HB 978 1 40835 825 2   PB 978 1 40835 826 9

Printed and bound in China

Orchard Books
An imprint of Hachette Children's Group
Part of The Watts Publishing Group Limited
Carmelite House, 50 Victoria Embankment, London EC4Y 0DZ

An Hachette UK Company
www.hachette.co.uk   www.hachettechildrens.co.uk

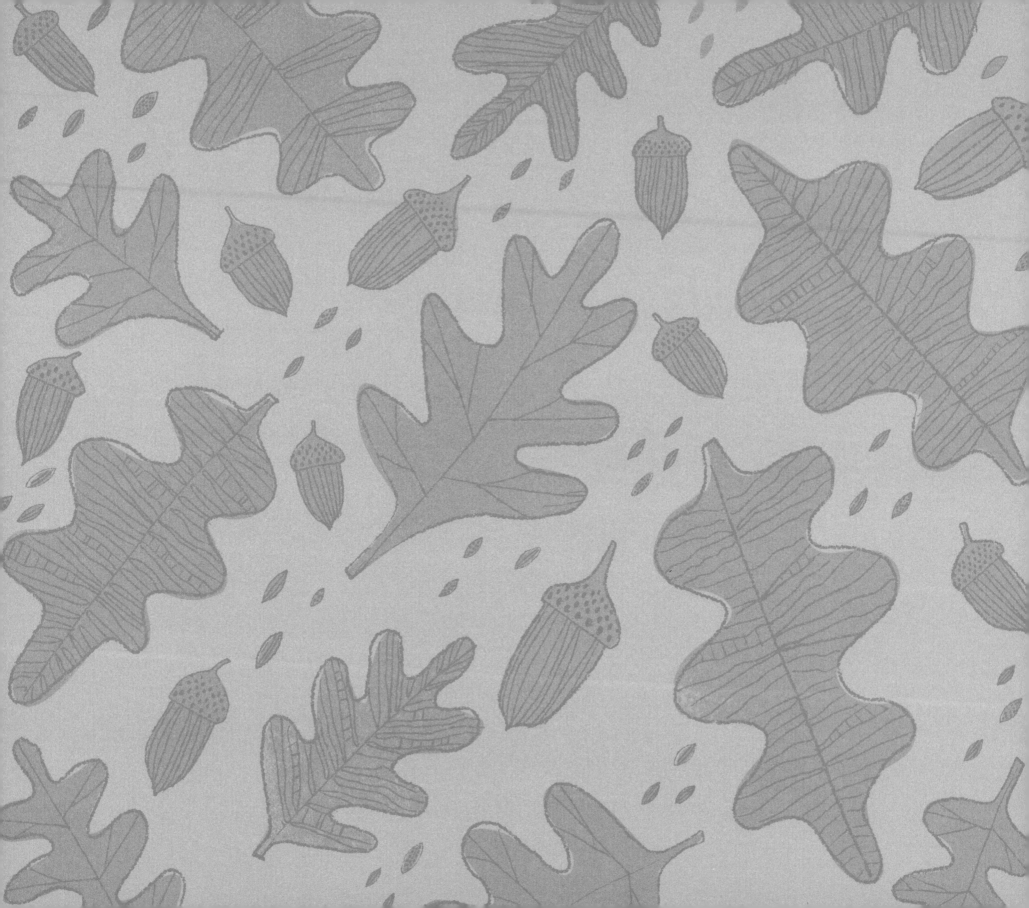